For every nanna
with a button tin
D. W.

A heart
with stories secured within
So too
my nanna's button tin
H. P.

First U.S. edition 2018

Library of Congress Catalog Card Number pending
ISBN 978-0-7636-8096-1

18 19 20 21 22 23 APS 10 9 8 7 6 5 4 3 2 1

Printed in Humen, Dongguan, China

This book was typeset in Mrs. Eaves.
The illustrations were done in gouache.

Candlewick Press
99 Dover Street
Somerville, Massachusetts 02144

visit us at www.candlewick.com

Nanna's Button Tin

Dianne Wolfer illustrated by Heather Potter

CANDLEWICK PRESS

I love Nanna's button tin. It's full of stories.

I take off the lid and tip it upside down.
Buttons tumble onto the floor.

The buttons are all shapes and sizes.
Nanna and I spread them out.

We need a special button for Teddy.

We start sorting the buttons.
The button I'm looking for
needs to be just the right size,
just the right shape, and just
the right color.

Nanna holds up a
tiny yellow circle.
"This one is special,"
she says. "It was on the
jacket you wore home
from the hospital."

The button is shiny-bright, but
it's not the right one for Teddy.

Nanna shows me a
button shaped like a bear.
"I remember that button," I say.
"It was on the birthday sweater
you made me. With this
button . . . and this one."

"Three bears for a girl
turning three." Nanna laughs.
"Now you'd need six buttons!"
I smile and put down the bear.
It isn't the one for Teddy.

We search

and sort

and search again.

Teddy looks sad.
"Don't worry," I say.
"I'm sure we'll find
just the right one."

Nanna holds a sparkly
green button. "This was
on the dress I wore when
I first met Pop. He said the
buttons matched my eyes."

We move the green button
aside. It's pretty, but it isn't
the right button for Teddy.
He needs a brown one.

I hold up a silver button.
"Tell me about this one," I ask.
"One winter you were very sick," Nanna whispers.
"Your mother sewed angel buttons onto each corner
of a blanket. She hoped they'd help keep you safe."

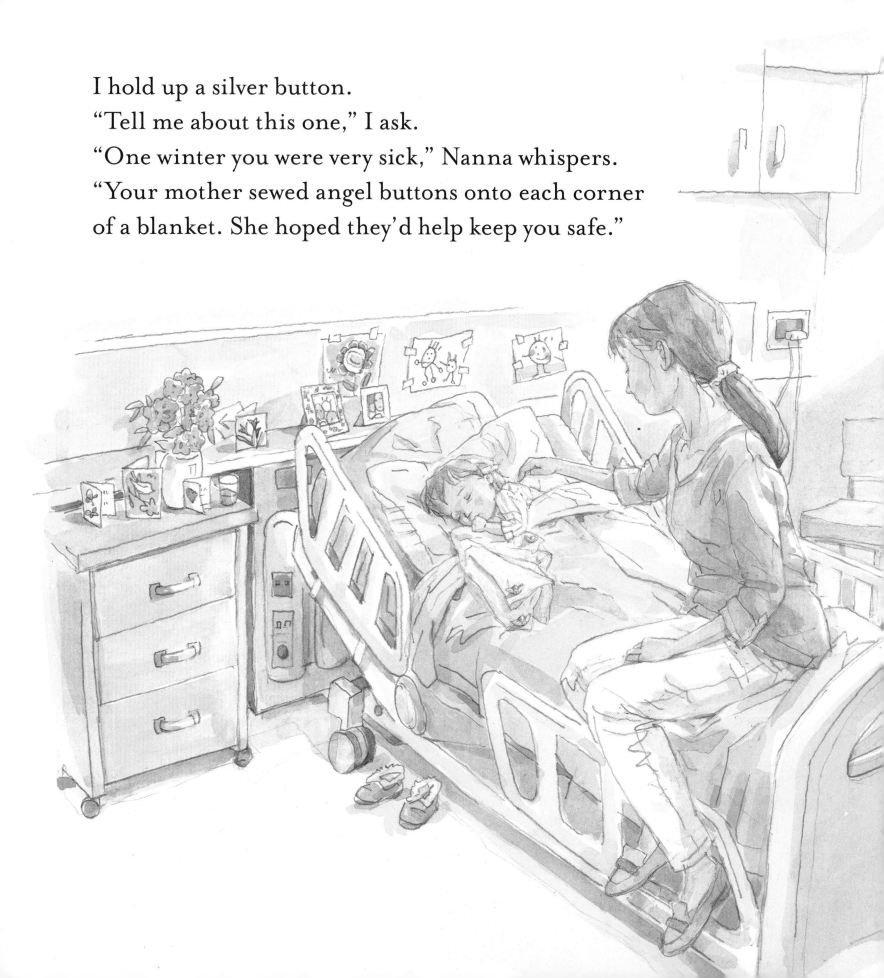

"And they did," I say,
spreading my arms into
angel wings. "But I don't
think Teddy needs an angel."
We keep looking.

At last I see a small brown circle. It's tucked
between the blues and the greens.

It's the right size and
the right shape. And I think
it's the right color. . . .

Teddy winks as I hand the button to Nanna.
"Perfect," she says, threading her needle.
"A perfect brown button for a perfect brown bear."

I hold Teddy tight while Nanna sews.
"Once upon a time," I tell him,
"there was a very brave bear. One day
he was cuddled so hard that he lost an eye."

"The teddy had a big operation," Nanna says
as she sews the last stitch. "And then . . .

"he was as good as new."

I kiss Teddy and squeeze his paw.
Then we gather Nanna's buttons
and put them back into their tin,
ready for next time.